Echoes Across Worlds

ECHOES ACROSS WORLDS

First edition. April 22, 2024.

ISBN: 979-8224012312

Written by NM Mal.

Prologue

In the heart of Aria, the huge Solarian city where towering buildings rose to the heavens and glowing paths ran through the cityscape like veins of light, there was a division deeper than the sparkling towers. Beyond the city gates, there was a dramatic contrast to the Solarians' richness and majesty.

The Lunarians lived in the ancient forests beyond Aria, where the trees murmured stories of time everlasting and the earth held the memories of centuries before. They were a people that lived in harmony with nature, their lives linked with the seasonal changes of the wilderness.

For decades, the Solarians and Lunarians had coexisted as adjacent worlds but prejudice and fear had severed their relationship. The Solarians, with their advances in technology and money, saw the Lunarians as rustic outsiders who adhered to ancient traditions. The Lunarians, in turn, saw the Solarians as distant and disconnected, their town a beacon of excess founded on exploitation.

Against this backdrop of hatred and isolation, fate told a different story. Aria, a vibrant young artist of Lunarian origin, had a longing for adventure that extended beyond the confines of her forest home. Eron, heir to the prestigious Solarian dynasty, had ambitions tempered by an unconscious need for significance outside the constraints of his privileged upbringing. Their paths crossed one fateful day, setting off a chain of events that would shake the very foundation of their divided society. Aria and Eron, drawn together by an unexplained kinship, dared to break the harsh standards and expectations that had separated their worlds.

As the stars aligned and fate beckoned, Aria and Eron stood on the verge of change, their love echoing across opposing realms. But little did they realize that their union would resurrect ancient prophecies and unleash powers that wanted to either separate or unite their divided world.

Aria and Eron's mission to reinvent the very essence of their worlds was set in motion by this story of love and defiance, of togetherness against all odds. Through struggles and tribulations, loss and discovery, they would attempt to bridge the gap between Solarians and Lunarians, kindling a flame of hope that would light up the shadows of divide and usher in a new era of understanding.

Chapter 1: The Encounter

The murmur of imagination and the shimmer of false light filled the air on the crowded streets of Aria, the Solarian city's heart. Tall glass and steel towers rose higher, providing many-sided shady zones on the ground below. Aria, a young woman with chestnut hair and a brilliance in her eyes, weaved her way through the crowds, her material bag trailing behind her and her mind lost in thoughts of varieties and architectures.

As Aria turned a corner into a more peaceful alleyway, she paused to draw the silhouette of a distant building against the twilight sky. Lost in her artistic reverie, she missed the figure arriving from the opposite direction—a young man clothed in good Solarian clothes, his demeanour introspective. Eron was the heir to one of Aria's wealthiest and most powerful families.

Their collision was sudden and gentle, with their eyes meeting in amazement. Eron instinctively reached out to stabilise Aria as her sketches scattered like autumn leaves in the wind. "I'm terribly sorry," he murmured, his voice quiet and curious. Aria blinked, flustered by the experience. "No injury done," she said, her cheeks flushed slightly. She bent to recover her scattered sketches, and Eron knelt beside her, his gaze drawn to the bright drawings. "You have a talent for capturing the essence of our city," he said, his tone reflecting adoration.

Regardless of their social rank, Aria sensed a strange connection with Eron - one that opposed the apparent barriers that separated their realms. She grinned, a hint of mischief in her eyes. "Maybe you'll pose for me someday in the not-too-distant future," she remarked enthusiastically, and Eron's lips curved into a true grin, surprising even himself.

Their conversation continued, weaving through both everyday and deep topics. Aria learnt about Eron's childhood inside the lavish walls of the Solarian world class, while Eron listened intently as Aria told stories about Lunarian life beyond the city. Every confession broke down any barriers between their universes, leaving them both feeling intrigued and amazed.

As dusk crept over the city of Aria, Eron sincerely excused himself, promising to look for Aria's artwork at the city's galleries. Aria felt a flutter of eagerness as she watched him depart into the labyrinth of city life, fascinated by the collision of two conflicting worlds.

Chapter 2: Forbidden Bonds

Aria couldn't get Eron out of her mind in the days after their unforeseen encounter. His presence lingered like a wisp of a forgotten tune, elusive but enticing. Despite her parents' cautions about the risks of mingling with Solarians, Aria's curiosity and developing attraction for Eron drove her down a path she knew was loaded with risk.

Meanwhile, Eron was dealing with his own mixed emotions. Raised in the strict expectations of Solarian society, he was well aware of the consequences of pursuing a relationship with someone from the Lunarian borders. His mother, a powerful matriarch with her own goals, would never support such a match, seeing it as a danger to their family's prestigious status.

One evening, amid the canopy of stars that covered the sky above Aria's forest home, she told her parents about her experiences with Eron. Their expressions clouded with anxiety, and lines of worry appeared on their aged faces. "Aria, you must understand the divide between our worlds," her father warned, his voice grave. "The Solarians see us as inferior human beings, undeserving of their respect." Aria's mother put a soothing hand on her daughter's shoulder. "Your heart may yearn for him, but the consequences could be awful," she said quietly. Aria nodded, her eyes brimming with purpose. "But what if we could change things?" she questioned, her eyes bright with excitement. "What if our love could unite the divide?"

Meanwhile, amid the great halls of the Solarian estate, Eron became entangled in a web of familial responsibilities and expectations. His mother, Lady Elara, a woman of immaculate grace and unwavering control, invited him to her apartment one evening. "Eron, I've heard whispers of your recent adventures," she said calmly, her sharp eyes locked on him. "Do not forget your responsibilities to our family." Lunarians are not to be trifled with.

Eron gulped hard, a sense of contempt swelling within him. "Mother, I've found something... someone," he said, trembling somewhat under his mother's intense gaze. "Aria," he confessed, the word lingering like a forbidden secret on his tongue.

Lady Elara's countenance stiffened, her features as rigid as stone. "You will cut all ties with this Lunarian girl," she demanded, her voice cutting through the silence like a pointed razor. "Our family's integrity is at stake."

But Eron's heart refused to follow his mother's orders. As the days grew into nights and their secret meetings continued, he found himself lured deeper into Aria's world—one of simplicity, honesty, and unrestricted desire. Aria, in turn, saw a side of Eron that contradicted his royal persona, discovering a kindred spirit beneath the facade of luxury and expectation.

Despite the threat of societal rejection, Aria and Eron's friendship grew deeper, propelled by the forbidden thrill of their relationship. They spent time together in hidden spaces and quiet nooks, sharing hopes and aspirations that went beyond the confines of their split worlds. With each stolen glimpse and murmured vow, they dared to defy the standards that attempted to keep them apart.

Chapter 3: Secret Meetings

As their secret encounters continued, Aria and Eron found peace in the moments they were able to spend away from society's scrutiny. Each meet up was a beautiful ballet of forbidden love, with their chats creating an ensemble of shared dreams and goals. They discovered a haven in the shadows of the noisy Solarian city, a place where their world's preconceptions were rendered insignificant.

One afternoon, Aria took Eron on a journey outside the city boundaries, into the outskirts, where the rich beauty of the Lunarian forests welcomed them like an old friend. Eron gazed at the wild beauty that surrounded them, the ancient trees echoing stories of lost knowledge. Together, they walked meandering roads and discovered secluded forest areas, Aria telling stories about her youth in nature's embrace.

In exchange, Eron introduced Aria to the wonders of Solarian technology, a world of breathtaking creations and unlimited potential. They went through interactive galleries and colourful marketplaces, Eron's eyes beaming with pride as he demonstrated the glories of his planet. Aria, for her part, took in the sight with astonishment and curiosity, admiring the creativity that marked the Solarian way of life.

Despite their dissimilar backgrounds, Aria and Eron discovered common ground in their need for knowledge and connection. They talked about art, literature, and philosophy, their minds interweaving like ivy strands on ancient ruins. Each encounter was a revelation, demonstrating the transformational power of empathy and real friendship.

However, as the days passed, a cloud of uncertainty hung over their growing connection. Aria couldn't help but detect a tension in Eron's manner whenever they discussed their future. "What do you fear, Eron?" she inquired one evening, her gaze searching. Eron hesitated, feeling the weight of unspoken facts. "My mother... she is determined to keep us apart," he said, his tone filled with sadness.

Aria's heart tightened at the mention of Lady Elara, knowing all too well the strong obstacle she posed to their happiness. "We cannot let fear determine our fate," Aria stated, her eyes full of conviction. "Together, we can overcome the expectations that seek to isolate us."

Eron's determination was reignited after being inspired by Aria's unwavering conviction. He resolved to stick by her side, even as criticism resonated through the halls of his family's home. "We will find a way," he told Aria, his voice a gentle assurance among the stormy sea of unease.

Their love, once a secret affair, now shone brilliantly, a light of hope in the darkness of their split worlds. As they pushed farther into unfamiliar territory, Aria and Eron accepted the idea that their relationship was more than a temporary fancy—it was a monument to the enduring power of love, capable of breaking down the walls imposed by society's limited vision. And with each stolen moment, they renewed their commitment to one another, pressing forth on a path lit by the light of their shared dreams.

Chapter 4: Unveiling Secrets

As the days passed, Aria and Eron's bond grew stronger, but so did the weight of Eron's family legacy. Eron was haunted by his mother's stern warnings and the impending expectations of his ancestry, which caused him to feel uneasy. One evening, unable to suppress his inner agony, Eron sought comfort in Aria's wooded hideaway.

Eron shared his deepest anxieties to Aria in the midst of rustling leaves and nature's beautiful symphony. "My family... there are skeletons buried within our history," he continued, his voice filled with fear. Aria listened with a mixture of concern and unflinching support. Eron spoke of shadows that lingered in the halls of power, murmurs of a division that cut through their ancestors.

In that moment of vulnerability, Aria's heart went out to Eron. "Whatever it is, we will face it together," she reassured him, her voice a firm anchor in the maelstrom of uncertainty. Eron nodded, thankfulness imprinted on his face. For the first time in his privileged life, he felt the weight of expectation lift slightly, giving way to the growing hope that love could transcend even the darkest secrets.

Eron, determined to uncover the mysteries of his family's past, searched into ancient records and lost books in search of information that would cast light on the shadows that tormented him. Aria stayed by his side, her steadfast support being an indicator of strength in the maze of mystery. Together, they found bits of history—of alliances formed and broken, of betrayals and forgotten pledges.

One fateful evening, amongst the flickering glow of candles, Eron came across a revelation that rocked him to the core. In the yellowed pages of an old document, he saw a name—a name that rang through Solarian history like a haunting repetition. "My ancestor... he was responsible for the rift," Eron said, his voice tinged with scepticism.

Aria's eyes widened with awareness, and her mind raced to connect the connections. "What does this mean for us?" she inquired, her voice barely above whispering. Eron's eyes were fixed and his determination unshakable. "It means that we have the ability to rewrite our destiny," he stated, his voice filled with fresh determination.

As they explored deeper into the mysteries of Eron's family history, evil forces moved in the shadows, threatening to shatter their delicate dreams. Lady Elara, sensing a shift in her son's devotion, tightened her hold on the reigns of authority, her ambitions surpassing any sense of pity or compassion. Aria and Eron became entangled in a web of mystery, their love a beacon of rebellion amidst the schemes of those seeking to maintain the status norm.

Amidst the stormy currents of change, Aria and Eron clung to each other like sailors in a storm, their hearts connected in a vision of a world free of prejudice and fear. They faced the storm of uncertainty together, and their love is a monument to the human spirit's resilience—a spirit capable of overcoming even the darkest shadows of history.

Chapter 5: The Escape

As the pressure from Eron's family mounted, Aria and Eron recognized they needed to take immediate action to protect their relationship. With determination burning in their hearts, they took a brave decision: to flee the claustrophobic walls of the Solarian city and seek refuge among the Lunarians, where they hoped to be safe from Eron's mother and her accomplices.

Aria and Eron fled the luxurious house at night, leaving behind a life rooted in tradition and expectation. Their trip through the outskirts of Aria was packed with anxiety and uncertainty, but their determination drove them forward. As they proceeded deeper into the wilderness, Aria's expertise with the landscape served as a guiding light, taking them to the heart of the Lunarian forests.

Eron experienced an epiphany when he moved from the frenetic downtown to the serene embrace of nature. The air was alive with the sound of chirping birds and rustling plants, in stark contrast to the robotic buzz of Solarian technology. Aria smiled as Eron's eyes expanded in surprise, his spirit free of society standards.

Aria's family greeted them warmly in the middle of the Lunarian forest, where they lived in a simple cottage surrounded by tall trees and lush vegetation. Eron gazed at their simple way of life, the lack of excess a monument to the Lunarian spirit of natural harmony. Aria's parents accepted Eron like one of their own, and their hospitality soothed his tired soul.

As the days passed into weeks, Aria and Eron found comfort in the peaceful routine of Lunarian life. They tended the farm, gathered herbs for healing potions and told stories around the fire.

Away from the watchful eyes of Solarian society, their love sprang like wildflowers in the meadow, uncontrolled and beautiful.

Yet, even in their newfound shelter, Eron's conscience was haunted by past events. He struggled with the weight of his family's past, troubled by the discovery of his ancestor's wrongdoings. Aria stood at his side, a rock of unflinching support, her love a ray of hope amid the dark.

One evening, amid the moonlight, Eron confided in Aria about his inner anguish. "I fear that my mother's influence extends even into these sacred woods," he admitted, his voice coated with anxiety. Aria tenderly grasped his palm, her eyes wide with empathy. "Together, we will face whatever difficulties lie ahead," she declared, her voice firm.

Determined to carve out a future free of the shadows of the past, Aria and Eron formulated a strategy to confront Lady Elara and seek peace. They understood that returning to the Solarian city would mean facing terrible foes, but they refused to let fear control their fate. With fresh purpose, they set out on a trip back to Aria, equipped with the strength of their love and the tenacity of their spirits.

As they approached the next chapter, Aria and Eron realised that their love survived the difficulties of separation and uncertainty, rising stronger and more solid than ever. Together, they would defy expectations and pave the way for a future where love had no bounds—a future lighted by their unwavering commitment.

Chapter 6: Trials In The Wilderness

Aria and Eron discovered a paradise of simplicity and natural beauty deep within the lush Lunarian woodlands. Surrounded by tall trees and the serene symphony of bird songs, they accepted a life far apart from the wealth and aspirations of the Solarian capital. Aria's family greeted Eron with open arms, not as a Solarian prince, but as a kindred spirit seeking comfort and understanding.

As the days stretched into weeks, Aria and Eron were engrossed in the routines of Lunarian life. They participated in communal gatherings under the night sky, sharing laughs and stories with Aria's family. Eron, formerly shackled by society conventions, found emancipation in their simple lifestyle—a life controlled not by wealth or power, but by harmony with nature and communal relationships.

Aria guided Eron through Lunarian traditions, teaching him how to search for wild herbs and weave intricate patterns into natural fibre garments. Eron admired Aria's creativity and resilience, her connection to the soil demonstrating the strength of her spirit.

Aria and Eron's love bloomed like wildflowers in the meadow, surrounded by the tranquillity of their forest retreat. They spent stolen moments by the riverside, hands interlaced, watching the water flow over smooth pebbles. Eron found consolation in Aria's presence, and her unfailing support soothed his tormented soul.

Despite the calm exterior, Eron's thoughts were filled with doubts. The weight of his family's past haunted him, a continual reminder of the difficulties they would confront when they returned to the Solarian capital. Aria felt his inner struggle and offered reassurance, her voice a soothing melody among the natural music.

Aria and Eron travelled deep into the woods one evening, as the setting sun shed a golden glow over the forest canopy, in search of a hidden clearing known only to the Lunarian elders. Aria's father told stories of strength and unity passed down through generations while surrounded by ancient trees and the soft rustling of the wind.

Listening to Aria's father's advice gave Eron a fresh feeling of purpose. He knew that their love was more than just a transient romance; it was a sign of hope, a light that may cross the gap between their worlds. With newfound courage, Eron is determined to confront his mother and pave the way for reconciliation, guided by the ageless wisdom of Lunarian elders.

As the moon rose high in the sky, casting a gleaming radiance over the woodland, Aria and Eron returned to their humble dwelling, their hearts filled with hope for a future moulded by togetherness and understanding. Together, they devised arrangements for their return to the Solarian city, their spirits bolstered by love and the Lunarians' lasting legacy.

Aria and Eron realised that love could transcend cultural rules and expectations in the peaceful embrace of the Lunarian forests. With each passing instant, they grew closer, their spirits intertwining like roots beneath the earth—a monument to love's transformational power in the face of tragedy. As they prepared to embark on the next chapter of their adventure, Aria and Eron accepted the uncertainties of the future, knowing that their love would guide them through the hardships that were ahead.

Chapter 7: Betrayal

As Aria and Eron basked in the peacefulness of Lunarian existence, a shadow of dread hung over them. Unbeknownst to them, Eron's brother, Garret, nursed immense envy and contempt of Eron's feelings for Aria. Garret, driven by personal goals, saw Aria as a barrier to his rise within Solarian society.

One fateful day, as Aria and Eron walked deeper into the jungle, Garret's duplicity was revealed. A group of Solarian enforcers dedicated to Garret's cause stormed on Aria's family's homestead, disrupting the serene peace of the Lunarian refuge. Aria's family, caught off surprise, fought fiercely to keep their guests safe, but the odds were stacked against them.

Eron, sensing danger, dashed back to the homestead, Aria by his side. Their hearts hammered with fear as they arrived to discover turmoil and ruin. Aria's father lay wounded, his face marked with anger as he fought Garret's enforcers. Aria's mother, her eyes filled with unflinching determination, defended her family with unwavering courage.

In a moment of desperation, Eron addressed Garret, their gazes locked in a quiet struggle of will. "This madness ends now, Garret," Eron stated, his voice ringing with conviction. Garret's stare was filled with hatred, his betrayal engraved into the wrinkled lines of his brow.

Aria, her heart heavy with pain, pleaded for reason in the midst of turmoil. "Garret, why?" she asked, her voice shaking with shock. Garret's laughter was flat, without sorrow. "You were always the favoured one, Eron," his words tinged with malice. "It's time for a new era in Solarian society—one where I hold the reins of power."

As the standoff neared a climax, Aria and Eron discovered the extent of Garret's deceit. With Aria's family in danger and the sanctity of the Lunarian shelter destroyed, Eron's determination hardened like steel. "You will not win, Garret," he promised, his voice low in the middle of chaos. Aria stood by his side, her eyes filled with unshakable determination.

In a moment of clarity, Eron summoned the last shreds of Solarian honour within his brother, pleading for reason among the turmoil.

Chapter 8: Alliance

Following Garret's betrayal, Aria's family faced a terrible reality: their formerly serene haven was now polluted by the threat of Solarian assault. Aria's father and mother tended to their wounds, unshaken by the havoc caused by Garret's enforcers.

Eron, filled with guilt and determination, swore to make amends for his brother's betrayal. He sought advice from reliable allies in the Solarian city—people who shared his goal of harmony and justice. They devised a plan to expose Garret's plans and gather sympathetic elements behind their cause.

Meanwhile, Aria attended to the needs of her family, her heart burdened with concern for their safety. She gained strength from Eron's constant support, his presence a ray of hope in the middle of the approaching gloom. They discussed their next step, determined to bring peace to their shattered society.

In a bold act of defiance, Eron addressed his mother, Lady Elara, in the halls of their family home. "Garret's conduct cannot go unpunished," he stated, his voice full of authority. Lady Elara, caught aback by her son's commitment, struggled with conflicting emotions: devotion to her family's legacy with an urge for justice.

Eron pleaded with his mother to cooperate, appealing to her sense of honour and responsibility. "We must unite Solarian and Lunarians alike to overcome the divisions that threaten to tear us apart," he begged, his words resonating with generations past. Lady Elara's hard demeanour faltered as she regarded her son's heartfelt plea.

As Aria's family recovered under Eron's watchful gaze, a wave of change exploded through the Solarian city. Disappointed by Garret's brash ambition and the crimes perpetrated in his name, sympathetic factions banded together to support Eron. Aria saw the seeds of togetherness emerging and sensed a glimpse of hope in the middle of the chaos.

Eron's efforts paid off when Solarian and Lunarian supporters banded together for a similar goal: to disclose the truth and restore balance to their divided nation. They revealed Garret's treason to the Solarian council, exposing the corruption that existed throughout their ranks.

Garret's activities were uncovered, and he faced severe vengeance from the Solarian authorities. Aria's family, appreciative for Eron's unwavering support, expressed deep appreciation to him and his allies. Eron, moved by their gratitude, committed to work for a future of love and unity.

As the dust settled and the scars of betrayal began to heal, Aria and Eron stood side by side, their hearts joined in the pursuit of a better future. They enjoyed a calm moment amidst the chaos, their eyes reflecting the strength of their emotions. They envisioned a world in which conflicting worlds could coexist peacefully, formed by the transformational power of love and unity.

Chapter 9: Revelations

As the dust settled and the scars of betrayal began to heal, Aria and Eron stood side by side, their hearts joined in the pursuit of a better future. They enjoyed a calm moment amidst the chaos, their eyes reflecting the strength of their emotions. They envisioned a world in which conflicting worlds could coexist peacefully, formed by the transformational power of love and unity.

Aria and Eron began on a series of diplomatic missions, organising meetings and cultural exchanges to develop mutual respect and appreciation. They demonstrated the beauty of Lunarian customs and the inventiveness of Solarian technology, proving that diversity can be a source of strength rather than separation.

As their efforts gained traction, Eron's mother, Lady Elara, reluctantly accepted her son's vision for a more inclusive society. Eron's defiance damaged her pride, but she saw greatness in his leadership. She reluctantly offered her support, but with a wary eye and a lingering sense of mistrust.

Aria's family was instrumental in the reconciliation movement, serving as representatives of Lunarian culture and creating links of friendship with Solarian allies. Aria's father, who has recovered from his injuries, presented eloquent lectures on the value of mutual tolerance and environmental responsibility that resonated with audiences from both sides.

Despite the advances accomplished, areas of resistance remained throughout Solarian society—diehard traditionalists who held onto outdated preconceptions and concerns. Eron, unfazed by the barriers, continued to advocate for his cause, addressing opponents with empathy and tolerance. Aria stood at his side, her steadfast support demonstrating their shared dedication to a better future.

Aria and Eron relished the simple pleasures of company in the quiet hours between their diplomatic activities. They explored the Solarian city's hidden corners, uncovering neglected gardens and antique monuments that bore witness to centuries of history. Each discovery strengthened their bond and reinforced their confidence in the revolutionary power of love.

During the swirl of change, Eron confided in Aria about his plans for their future. "I envision a world where our children can grow up without the shadows of division," he said, his voice full of hope. Aria's heart overflowed with love and adoration for Eron, sharing his vision of a future where love triumphed all.

As their power widened, Aria and Eron were propelled into positions of leadership, their voices ringing through the halls of authority. Together, they fought for policies that encouraged equality and cooperation, challenging long-held ideas and paving the path for a society with greater diversity.

Despite the hardships that lay ahead, Aria and Eron remained committed to each other and their shared purpose. They were aware that the journey to long-term change would be difficult, but they found strength in the unbreakable link they had formed—a bond that surpassed the borders of their opposing worlds and paved the path to a brighter tomorrow.

Chapter 10: The Prophecy

Following their diplomatic efforts, Aria and Eron became leaders of a growing movement for Solarian and Lunarian unity and understanding. Their campaign touched people from all walks of life, instilling hope and developing a feeling of shared purpose. Aria and Eron set out on an epic journey to reshape the fabric of their world as they stood on the verge of change.

Lady Elara, Eron's mother, cautiously accepted her son's vision for a more open society, acknowledging the inevitability of change. Though her pride remained seething beneath the surface, she began to play an important role in bridging the divide between Solarian traditionalists and modern reformers. Her influence swayed major members of the Solarian council, setting the stage for broad reforms that would reshape the norms of society.

Aria's family, proud representatives of Lunarian culture, stood with Eron and Lady Elara, joining the chorus of change. Aria's father, a symbol of wisdom and endurance, offered stirring talks about unity and environmental conservation. Aria's mother, a compassionate figure, formed strong links with Solarian allies, creating friendships that transcended previous biases.

As their movement gained traction, Aria and Eron faced increasing pressure from opponents who clung to dated ideals. They faced resistance at every turn, yet they remained constant in their belief that love and understanding were the keys to a better future. They withstood the storm of hostility together, with their love serving as an anchor in the midst of rough seas.

In the quiet hours between public appearances, Aria and Eron found comfort in each other's arms. They stole moments of peace amidst the city's chaos, enjoying stolen kisses and whispered vows. Aria's laughter was like music to Eron's ears, drowning out the commotion of doubt and uncertainty.

Eron took Aria by the hand one evening and led her to a secret rooftop garden hidden from society's prying eyes, lit by the shimmering light of a Solarian moon. Eron dropped to one knee, surrounded by the aroma of blooming flowers and the soft glow of lanterns, his eyes glinting with determination. "Aria, you are my guiding light, my partner on this journey," he said quietly, his voice full of passion.

Aria's heart skipped a beat as Eron gifted her a bright gemstone, a legacy passed down through centuries of Solarian royalty. "Will you stand by my side as my equal, my love, as we continue to forge a path towards unity and understanding?" Eron inquired, his voice full of optimism. Aria, overcome with emotion, nodded passionately, her eyes filled with tears of ecstasy.

Aria and Eron announced their engagement to a world on the verge of change. Their union represented more than simply love; it embodied the spirit of reconciliation and the prospect of a common future. In the days that followed, festivities resonated through Aria's streets, bringing Solarians and Lunarians together in a joyful demonstration of unity.

Among the merriment, Aria and Eron had moments of quiet meditation to appreciate the gravity of their devotion to each other and their mission. They knew their road hadn't ended, but they approached the future with unyielding determination, their hearts connected like threads in a tapestry of hope. Together, they would continue to defend the values of unity and understanding, paving the way for a world in which love knew no bounds.

Chapter 11: Trials Of Unity

As Aria and Eron's engagement signalled a new era of faith and solidarity, the planning for their wedding became a symbol of peace between Solarians and Lunarians. The city of Aria was alive with enthusiasm, with flags showing entwined emblems of two worlds—a sun and a crescent moon—a monument to the union that had transcended ancient barriers. Aria's family collaborated tirelessly with Solarian artists to create a celebration that reflected the beauty of both cultures.

Eron, now fully involved in his role as a visionary leader, continued to advocate for legislation that encouraged equality and cooperation. He led measures to invest in Lunarian villages, providing resources for education and long-term development. Aria stood at his side, her steadfast support demonstrating their shared commitment to creating a better world.

Aria and Eron snuck peaceful moments together amidst the flurry of preparations, their love a strong anchor in the middle of it all. They retreated to private gardens and secret alcoves, enjoying stolen kisses and murmured vows. Aria's laughter echoed like music in Eron's ears, drowning out the cacophony of their busy surroundings.

As their wedding date approached, Aria's father gave wisdom to Eron, emphasising the value of kindness and compassion in leadership. Eron listened closely, his admiration for Aria's father growing with every passionate disclosure. Aria's mother gave Eron a beloved Lunarian heirloom—a moonstone pendant—as a symbol of acceptance and harmony.

On the eve of their wedding, Aria and Eron stood on a hill overlooking the city, Aria's glittering lights spreading out before them like an array of stars. "Tomorrow, we begin a new chapter together," Eron muttered, his gaze set on the horizon. Aria clasped his hand, her heart full with love and excitement.

The morning of their wedding began with bright skies and a sense of expectancy in the air. Aria wore a gown that combined Solarian beauty with Lunarian motifs—ivory silk embroidered with beautiful moonflowers—and was embellished with heirloom jewellery passed down through generations of lunarian women. Eron stood magnificent in Solarian clothing, a sign of the unity they wished to represent.

As Aria came down the aisle, accompanied by her delighted parents, the city held its breath in amazement of the union before them. Both Solarian and Lunarian visitors watched the conclusion of a love story that defied convention and broke down barriers. Aria and Eron exchanged vows filled with the promise of mutual respect and unwavering commitment, their voices a tribute to the strength of love in a divided world.

The party that followed was a brilliant weave of Solarian and Lunarian traditions—a feast of tastes, music, and dancing that highlighted the diversity of their shared ancestry. Aria's father gave a poignant address, evoking the spirit of unity and optimism that had guided their journey. Guests from both worlds mixed with joyous abandon, forming relationships that would last beyond the celebrations.

Aria and Eron slipped away from the festivities as the sun set and lights illuminated the night sky, their hearts full with thanks and joy. They looked into one other's eyes, their spirits joining in a commitment to continue their search for a world where love knew no bounds. Aria and Eron realised in that moment of calm joy, amidst the sound of celebration, that their love story was only just getting started—a narrative of tenacity, fortitude, and the transformational power of love.

Chapter 12: Loss

In the midst of Aria and Eron's joyful celebration and shared vision for a peaceful future, tragedy came unexpectedly, throwing a pall over their newfound pleasure. Aria's father, the acclaimed ambassador of Lunarian culture, demonstrated unprecedented bravery and sacrifice in front of dignitaries and sympathisers from both the Solarian and Lunarian communities.

As emotions rose and protestors attempted to disturb the festivities, Aria's father moved forward without hesitation, protecting Aria and Eron from harm. In a moment of heroic sacrifice, he confronted the intruders, his steadfast resolution a witness to the depth of his love for his daughter and the cause they supported.

Aria's heart crumbled as she observed her father's deed of courage, his life cut short in defence of their common ideal of unification. Eron, filled with grief and disbelief, clutched Aria close as turmoil erupted around them. The sounds of violence echoed through the air, mixed with cries of agony and yells of resistance.

Following the incident, Aria and Eron were left with enormous grief and a fresh sense of purpose. Aria's mother, her eyes filled with sadness but reinforced by resilience, pushed them to honour her husband's legacy by continuing their quest to challenge the status quo and bridge the gap between their worlds.

Eron's resolve was strengthened by the death of a mentor and father figure, and he promised to intensify his efforts in the struggle for justice and equality. He found refuge in Aria's unfailing support, her presence providing strength in the middle of an emotional storm. They drew solace from their shared recollections of Aria's father, a source of knowledge and compassion.

As they grieved their loss, Aria and Eron recognized that their quest for unification had become more essential and painful than ever. They turned their sadness into a fierce determination to battle the forces attempting to divide them, remembering Aria's father's sacrifice with unshakable commitment.

During the silent hours of grief, Aria's father's words rang in their hearts, guiding them forward. "The path to true unity requires courage and sacrifice," he had once told them, his voice deep with determination. Aria clung to his lessons, seeking comfort in the lasting legacy he left behind—a legacy that spurred their drive to defy the current quo.

In the midst of their sadness, Aria and Eron found solace in the support of their admirers and the solidarity of their communities. Solarian and Lunarian leaders joined in grief, putting aside their differences in the face of common loss. Together, they pledged to carry on Aria's father's vision, creating a future in which his sacrifice would not be in vain.

As Aria and Eron approached a new chapter in their journey, they were inspired by the strength of their love and the steadfast conviction that had brought them together. In the aftermath of tragedy, they discovered a new purpose—one based on hope, justice, and the lasting legacy of Aria's father's selfless sacrifice.

Chapter 13: The Rebellion

Following Aria's father's sacrifice and inspired by Aria and Eron's enduring love, whispers of rebellion spread like wildfire among the disaffected residents of both Solarian and Lunarian nations. Inspired by the couple's vision of unity and fairness, a movement arose—a revolt born of a shared desire for change and the belief that love could transcend boundaries.

Discontent boiled beneath the surface, as people excluded by society standards and biases found a voice in Aria and Eron's campaign. The poor and artisans, Lunarian tribespeople and Solarian labourers came together under a common banner of defiance, demanding an end to inequity and prejudice.

The uprising gathered traction as impassioned speeches resonated through Aria's streets, inspiring the underprivileged to oppose the entrenched authorities that fueled the divide. Aria and Eron, lauded as icons of hope and resilience, added their voices to the cause, urging togetherness and solidarity in the face of tragedy.

Despite the chaos of revolt, Aria's mother emerged as a beacon of leadership, guiding the disaffected with grace and resolve. Her compassion and wisdom struck a profound chord with the rebels, inspiring them to persevere in the face of adversity.

Eron, his heart heavy with responsibility, strategized with Aria and her mother on how to channel the rebellion's energy into positive change. They called for reforms that would break down structural barriers and promote true equality among Solarian and Lunarian citizens.

The insurrection spurred talks that crossed societal borders, generating a debate over every individual's inherent worth, regardless of birthplace or genealogy. Aria and Eron's love story became a rallying cry, demonstrating the transformational power of love to dismantle prejudice and encourage understanding.

As the rebellion increased in intensity, critics among the ruling class became increasingly concerned about the tide of change. Lady Elara, caught between loyalty to her ancestry and the desire to see her son happy, found herself at a crossroads, her allegiances tested by dramatic developments in Solarian culture.

Aria and Eron faced grave hurdles during the battle, with their love serving as a steadfast rock in the midst of chaos. They faced the challenges of insurrection with unyielding determination, their hearts connected with the rebels' cause of justice and togetherness.

As the revolt reached its peak, Aria and Eron stood on the verge of transformation, their hearts unified in the conviction that their love could spark change. They battled the forces of divide and injustice, inspired by a shared desire for a future in which love overcame everything.

Chapter 14: The Confrontation

In the midst of societal upheaval and insurrection, tensions between Eron's family and the insurgent rebels reached a boiling point, paving the way for a last, conclusive encounter. As Eron struggled with the weight of conflicting loyalties—his love for Aria and his familial duty—the fate of their universe hung in the balance.

The rebels, encouraged by Aria and Eron's unflinching commitment to justice, gathered their forces in the shadows, their resolve strengthened by the prospect of a brighter future. Aria, standing shoulder to shoulder with her fellow insurgents, exuded determination, her gaze set on the horizon of transformation.

Eron saw himself divided between opposing allegiances, his heart ripped apart by the imminent confrontation between his love for Aria and his duty to his heritage. Lady Elara, his mother, led Solarian soldiers, her stern resolve concealing a tempest of emotions beneath the surface.

As the conflict approached, Aria and Eron experienced a romantic moment of solace, taking refuge in each other's arms amidst the pandemonium. Aria's touch soothed Eron's worried spirit, and her unflinching trust in their love was a light of hope in the looming storm.

On the eve of war, Eron faced a critical decision: whether to stand at Aria's side and embrace the cause of justice, or to answer the call of duty and respect his family's legacy. The weight of his decision weighed hard on him, his emotions divided between the demands of his soul and the expectations of his bloodline.

As dawn came over the horizon, signifying the start of combat, Eron found himself at a crossroads, his determination hardening like a shard of hardened steel. He sought advice from Aria, and her steadfast support was a lifeline in the midst of uncertainty.

Solarian forces clashed with rebel insurgents in a climactic showdown, leaving echoes of battle throughout Aria. Amidst the pandemonium, Eron confronted his mother, Lady Elara, their eyes locked in wordless turmoil. Aria, her heart in her throat, waited with bated breath as the fate of their universe was in the balance.

Eron's voice broke through the din of battle, a tribute to the transformational power of love and unity. "Mother, I choose a future where love knows no boundaries," he declared, his voice firm. Lady Elara, her mask crumbling, confronted the depths of her son's conviction.

As the dust cleared and the echoes of combat faded, Aria and Eron stood amidst the ruins of battle, their hearts connected like vines in a forest of change. Together, they found a road forward, their love a light of hope in the wake of conflict.

Following the ultimate showdown, Aria and Eron emerged as forerunners of a new era—one in which love won over divide, justice reigned supreme, and the legacy of sacrifice and tenacity persisted. Together, they traversed the complexities of reconciliation, their hearts linked in the idea that their love could transform their world for future generations.

Chapter 15: Redemption

Following the violent battle between Solarian soldiers and rebels, Eron found himself at a crossroads, wrestling with the weight of his decisions and the ramifications for his future with Aria. As the dust settled, he approached his mother, Lady Elara, in a private chamber within their ancient estate. The air was thick with unsaid tension.

Eron, his heart heavy with resolution, approached Lady Elara with strong conviction, questioning the repressive customs that had long caused separation and injustice within Solarian society. "Mother, the time for change has come," he proclaimed, his voice full of determination. "We cannot continue to uphold outdated ideals that sow discord and perpetuate suffering."

Lady Elara's hard veneer faltered for a minute as she met Eron's gaze with pride and trepidation. She struggled to come to terms with her son's rebellion with her own firmly held convictions, split between familial devotion and a wish for a better future.

In a moment of crisis, Eron acknowledged the depth of his devotion to Aria and their shared aim for unity. He urged Lady Elara to believe in the transformational power of love and understanding, to stand on the right side of history and lead the road for peace between Solarians and Lunarians.

Aria stood by Eron's side as he spoke from the heart, her presence a mute monument to their unwavering love and commitment. They reflected the aspiration for a future in which difference gave way to solidarity, oppression to justice.

Lady Elara felt a surge of sympathy and understanding as she witnessed her son's unshakeable conviction and Aria's unyielding love. She saw in Eron's eyes a reflection of her own desire for a world free of prejudice and bigotry.

In a moment of redemption, Lady Elara made a decision that would change the direction of Solarian history. She embraced Eron and Aria, her heart laden with regret but lightened by the prospect of reconciliation. They swore to destroy the oppressive customs that had separated their community, ushering in a new era of collaboration and mutual respect.

The news of Lady Elara's change of heart spread like wildfire throughout the Solarian city, instilling hope in the disadvantaged and inspiring others to defy the established quo. Eron and Aria's example inspired the oppressed to rally even more passionately behind their cause.

As a new era dawned, Eron and Aria led the way toward reconciliation, their hearts united in the notion that love could overcome all difficulties. They worked together to construct a route forward, guided by the enduring heritage of sacrifice and redemption, paving the way for a society free of injustice and united in justice.

Chapter 16: Unity

After Lady Elara's dramatic change of heart and Eron's courageous stance against oppressive customs, the city of Aria buzzed with anticipation and optimism. Both Solarian and Lunarian citizens dared to trust in a future in which togetherness won over division, and love acted as a catalyst for long-term change.

Eron, encouraged by Aria and his mother's support, took on a leadership role within the Solarian council, calling for broad reforms that would break down institutional barriers and establish genuine cooperation between their nations. His passionate words captivated crowds across the city, inspiring others to join the cause of reconciliation.

Aria, her heart full of love and adoration for Eron, stood by his side as a steadfast companion in their joint objective. They managed the complexities of governing with elegance and determination, their love shining as a light of hope in the face of future obstacles.

Meanwhile, the rebels, energised by recent occurrences, focused their efforts on constructive programs aimed at reconstructing their villages and creating interaction between Solarian and Lunarian residents. Aria became a melting pot of ideas and aspirations, propelled by a sense of community and collaboration.

As Eron and Aria's influence expanded, so did pushback from established elements inside Solarian society. Traditionalists, fearful of change, planned in the shadows to impede the march toward reconciliation. Despite the challenges in his road, Eron remained steady in his resolve.

Eron and Aria went on a series of diplomatic trips to adjacent Solarian cities and Lunarian settlements, extending olive branches of peace and building alliances that overcame ancient animosities in a symbolic gesture of unification. Their efforts paid off as bridges were created and walls were demolished, paving the way for a more integrated world.

In the midst of the diplomatic frenzy, Eron and Aria sought refuge in secret gardens and hidden alcoves, where they could savour stolen kisses and murmured vows. Aria's laughter was a symphony that rang through Eron's emotions, drowning out the cacophony of their crowded surroundings.

As the city of Aria grew under their leadership, Eron and Aria were welcomed into their communities. They held cultural exchanges that highlighted the diversity of Solarian and Lunarian traditions, promoting mutual understanding and admiration.

In the quiet hours of introspection, Eron confided in Aria about his aspirations and dreams for their shared future—a future in which their love serves as the foundation of a society founded on equality and compassion. Aria listened intently, her emotions filled with love and admiration for the guy who had captured her heart.

Eron and Aria stood on the verge of a new chapter in their lives, their hearts linked in the idea that love could overcome any difficulty. As they looked into the horizon of potential, they realised that their love story was far from over—a story of tenacity, courage, and love's transforming power in crafting a world where unity reigned supreme.

Chapter 17: New Beginnings

The city of Aria soaked in the glory of newly discovered togetherness and growth, fuelled by Eron and Aria's unflinching commitment to reconciliation. Solarian and Lunarian inhabitants interacted freely on the streets, swapping stories and customs that celebrated their common ancestry. Festivals and cultural events became commonplace, creating a tapestry of diversity and mutual respect.

Eron, now an esteemed member of the Solarian council, continued to advocate for policies that promoted equality and collaboration. He worked with progressive leaders from both sides to enact reforms that addressed long-standing complaints and encouraged social harmony.

Aria was by Eron's side every step of the way, helping to bridge cultural barriers and foster empathy between the Solarian and Lunarian cultures. Her kindness and resilience served as a beacon for people seeking to create a better future.

In a symbolic act of unity, Eron and Aria travelled across the region, visiting villages and towns that had long been rejected. They listened to everyday individuals' issues, forming bonds and establishing trust through genuine communication.

As their influence expanded, Eron and Aria learned to navigate the challenges of governing with grace and resolve. They organised councils of Solarian and Lunarian leaders to promote collaboration on problems ranging from environmental sustainability to economic prosperity.

Aria's family continued to play an important role in the city's development, serving as representatives of Lunarian culture and campaigners for unity. Aria's father's legacy lives on via their relentless attempts to foster understanding and collaboration.

Despite the difficulties they encountered, Eron and Aria stayed devoted to their common ideal of a future where love crossed borders. They found strength in the support of their supporters and the tenacity of their communities, knowing that they were not alone in their search for a better future.

As the city of Aria thrived under their leadership, Eron and Aria stood out as beacons of hope in a divided world. They embodied the transformational power of love and unity, motivating others to consider the prospect of reconciliation and cooperation.

Chapter 18: Healing Wounds

The city of Aria continued to thrive under Eron and Aria's leadership, and there was a palpable sense of optimism and unity in the air. Solarian and Lunarian inhabitants worked together to reconstruct and revitalise their communities. The once-divided city now thrived with a renewed sense of cooperation and mutual respect.

Eron's influence in the Solarian council grew as he advocated for progressive legislation aimed at resolving systematic imbalances. He worked with innovative leaders from both sides to create policies that improved education, healthcare, and economic opportunity for all citizens.

Aria, ever the compassionate advocate, promoted cultural interactions that highlighted the rich texture of Solarian and Lunarian customs. Festivals and gatherings became treasured opportunities for unification, where shared experiences strengthened the relationships between communities.

In a brave step toward healing, Eron invited representatives from adjacent Solarian cities and Lunarian villages to a conference centred on cooperation and collaboration. The meeting facilitated communication and mutual understanding, paving the door for regional coalitions.

Aria's family continued to play an important role in promoting cross-cultural understanding by sponsoring events highlighting Lunarian customs and traditions. Prejudices were dissolved throughout these talks, and friendships emerged.

Despite their hectic schedules, Eron and Aria found solace in quiet times of togetherness. They retreated to peaceful gardens and picturesque landscapes to relax and reflect on their shared experience.

Lady Elara, Eron's mother, accepted her role as a change agent, utilising her influence to bridge gaps in Solarian society. Her change from a diehard conservative to a champion of reconciliation pushed others to confront their own preconceptions.

Eron and Aria's impact spread throughout the city, leaving an unforgettable mark on future generations. Their voyage symbolised the conviction that love could truly overcome all, paving the way for a society in which differences were celebrated and togetherness reigned supreme.

Chapter 19: Discoveries

Eron and Aria's efforts toward unity and reconciliation paid off and the city of Aria proceeded to grow into a symbol of hope and progress. Solarian and Lunarian citizens coexisted peacefully, with their common experiences promoting a sense of belonging and understanding. Streets that were previously divided by prejudice were now teeming with many cultures, mingling in a thriving tapestry of life. Despite the success, problems remained, as elements of resistance attempted to undermine the increasing sense of unity. Eron and Aria fought detractors with patience and determination, using their influence to fight toxic speech and encourage empathy.

Eron and Aria started on a goodwill trip around surrounding regions, extending invitations to collaborate and partner as a symbolic show of support. Their outreach initiatives created regional partnerships and laid the framework for long-term cooperation.

Aria's family continued to play a crucial role in developing understanding between Solarian and Lunarian societies. Aria's father's wisdom echoed through generations, sparking a new era of cultural interaction and respect for one another.

Lady Elara, Eron's mother, became a beloved figure in Solarian society, her transition from traditionalist to advocate for change motivating others to embrace advancement. Her influence in the Solarian council paved the path for major reforms.

As the community grew under their leadership, Eron and Aria's narrative became synonymous with fortitude and optimism. Their unwavering dedication to togetherness demonstrated the transformational power of love in removing boundaries and developing understanding.

Eron and Aria's legacy lived on in the hearts of Aria's residents, leaving an imprint on the fabric of their society. Their voyage exemplified the conviction that compassion and empathy could truly heal scars and pave the way for a future in which differences were celebrated and togetherness reigned.

Chapter 20: Challenges Ahead

Aria and Eron basked in the accomplishment of their efforts toward unification, filling the air with a mix of jubilation and expectation. However, despite the festive environment, rumours of political intrigue and external threats loomed on the horizon, putting a pall over their newfound riches.

As leaders of a new era, Aria and Eron had to navigate a complicated web of alliances and conflicts inside the Solarian council. Traditionalist elements, unwilling to adapt, attempted to undercut their progressive agenda by inciting discontent and spreading seeds of discord.

Eron, bolstered by previous wins, faced internal obstacles with steadfast tenacity. He rallied council allies to embrace big reforms while keeping an eye out for adversaries who wanted to profit from splits.

Aria, ever the diplomat, participated in delicate negotiations with neighbouring territories, hoping to strengthen regional alliances amid shifting political circumstances. External threats lurked on the horizon, requiring strategic thinking and meticulous planning. Meanwhile, Lady Elara, Eron's mother, came under fresh scrutiny from long-standing rivals within Solarian society. Her transition from traditionalist to change advocate earned her the ire of those who opposed advancement.

As foreign threats grew, Eron and Aria grasped the importance of vigilance and togetherness. They formed emergency committees to organise resources and plan responses to possible crises, putting their leadership to the test in the face of hardship.

Despite the obstacles ahead, Eron and Aria remained steadfast in their dedication to a vision of togetherness and justice. They were inspired by their communities' resiliency and the transformative power of love, and they persevered with steadfast commitment.

Chapter 21: Hope Renewed

Aria faced a watershed moment when Erons wife discovered a lost Lunarian item that promised to revolutionise technology and usher in a new era of sustainable energy. The discovery instilled new optimism in its residents, providing a practical solution to critical environmental issues.

Aria discovered the relic during an archeological journey to the city's outskirts, driven by her innate curiosity and love of travel. Aria was attracted by the item, a beautifully constructed device infused with Lunarian markings, which hinted at untold potential. After further examination, Aria discovered that the artefact contained the key to utilise renewable energy sources in previously imagined ways. Solarian scientists and Lunarian intellectuals worked together to uncover its secrets, embarking on a voyage of discovery that promised to alter their world.

As word spread about Aria's incredible discovery, excitement swept over the city like a wave of anticipation. Citizens from all walks of life united around the promise of renewable energy, picturing a future in which fossil fuel reliance became a thing of the past. Eron, seeing the artefact's transformative potential, led campaigns to integrate its technology into everyday life. Solar panels decorated rooftops, absorbing sunshine to power homes and businesses, while wind turbines dot the countryside, harnessing the strength of nature's forces.

Aria's family played an important role in solving the artefact's secrets, drawing on Lunarian wisdom passed down through the decades. Their collaboration with Solarian inventors fostered a resurgence of scientific research and technological innovation.

As the city adopted sustainable methods, Eron and Aria's leadership received international notice. Representatives from nearby regions travelled to Aria to see the wonders of renewable energy firsthand, hoping to replicate its success in their own communities.

Aria's residents' hearts soared with hope as they welcomed a future led by the promise of renewable energy. Eron and Aria's quest to a greener tomorrow exemplified the conviction that dedication and inventiveness could conquer any challenge, paving the way for a world where nature and society coexisted together.

Chapter 22: Betrayal Revisited

The city of Aria faced an unforeseen threat when a shadow from Eron's past emerged, casting uncertainty and mistrust on the pillars of unity and progress that had been meticulously established. A traitor, long assumed to be forgotten, reappeared with malicious motives, determined to undo everything Eron and Aria had worked so hard to establish. The traitor's unexpected entrance sent shockwaves across the city, eliciting whispers of betrayal and duplicity. Eron's face pinched in concern as he recalled unsettling memories from a long ago, when loyalties were tested and trust was broken.

Aria, her intuition as keen as ever, recognized the significance of the situation and stood by Eron's side, steadfast in her support. Together, they looked into Eron's background, determined to find the traitor's motivations and protect the future they had worked so hard to create.

As Eron and Aria probed deeper, they discovered a complex web of deception and intrigue that threatened to undermine the fragile unity they had built. The traitor's actions called into question the loyalty of those closest to them, putting their allies to the test.

As tensions rose, Eron and Aria gathered their forces, enlisting trusted advisors and allies to face the impending threat. They established emergency committees to strategize countermeasures to the traitor's malicious plots while keeping an eye out for prospective partners.

Aria's family, fierce advocates of Lunarian heritage, contributed their skills to the investigation, using their knowledge of old secrets to decipher the traitor's intentions. They collected together evidence that pointed to a conspiracy based on long standing rivalries and secret goals.

As locals wrestled with the uncomfortable discovery of betrayal, whispers of distrust mixed with a chorus of hope in the city centre. Eron and Aria, strong in their resolve, refused to give in to fear, deriving strength from the unflinching support of their communities.

As emotions rose, Eron faced the traitor in a dramatic battle that tested his morals and resolve. Aria stood by his side, a silent reminder of the love and unity that had kept them going through tragedy. In the aftermath of the showdown, long-buried truths surfaced, exposing the traitor's objectives and unravelling the web of lies. Eron and Aria emerged stronger than ever, their bond built in the fires of betrayal, a tribute to love's enduring strength and tenacity.

As the city Aria came to terms with its past, Eron and Aria's legacy stood as a beacon of hope in a world where trust and unity triumphed over betrayal and deception. They managed the challenges of leadership with elegance and drive, their hearts unified in the idea that love could overcome even the darkest shadows.

Chapter 23: Reckoning

As the city of Aria faced challenges and reckonings, Aria found herself challenged with her own deeply held prejudices, learning that meaningful transformation required personal reflection and sacrifice.

Aria's awakening began with a series of enlightening interactions that challenged her preconceived assumptions and preconceptions. She observed personally the tenacity and humanity of people from various origins, which prompted a change in her perspective.

One watershed event occurred during a community gathering, when Aria engaged in a deep conversation with a Solarian craftsman whose family had formerly been her rivals. Aria recognized common ground and an ambition for a better future during their conversation.

Aria struggled with remorse and shame as she thought of her experiences, which had impaired her judgement. She learned that accepting change meant admitting and tackling her own flaws.

Aria sought advice from her lover and confidant, Eron, who urged her to continue on a path of self-discovery and progress. Together, they travelled the city's varied areas, meeting people whose experiences shed light on the intricacies of societal divisions.

During her own reckoning, Aria encountered internal opposition, including the unpleasantness of confronting her own biases and accepting unfamiliar ideas. She sought comfort in the company of allies and mentors who pushed her to face hard facts.

In a transforming moment of vulnerability, Aria confronted her family's prejudiced legacy, having uncomfortable conversations with loved ones about the need for empathy and understanding. Her attempt to reconcile with her history paralleled the city's overall yearning for harmony.

Aria's commitment to encouraging inclusion and compassion in her community grew in tandem with her perspective. She became an outspoken champion for change, utilising her position to call out toxic discourse and promote empathy. Aria's personal progress inspired others, generating conversations and activities to promote dialogue and understanding. Her path to reconciliation became an element of the city's larger search for harmony and justice.

In the midst of social turmoil, Aria's development demonstrated the transformational potential of personal contemplation and empathy. Aria symbolised the concept that true progress meant facing the shadows of the past while also embracing the potential of a brighter future.

Chapter 24: The Unveiling

Eron had been working on a huge plan, and now that Aria was functioning smoothly, he decided to announce a vision for a unified society that combined creativity of Solarian technology with the timeless wisdom of Lunarian legacy. Against the backdrop of societal transition, Eron's idea offered a daring step toward a future in which unity and progress coexisted.

Eron's grand reveal was met with tremendous expectation, with inhabitants from all walks of life gathered in the city centre to see the merging of Solarian ingenuity and Lunarian wisdom. When Eron went onto the stage, the air was packed with excitement and intrigue, and his presence demanded attention.

With unflinching conviction, Eron offered an accurate depiction of a society powered by renewable energy and characterised by sustainable practices. Solarian engineers and Lunarian intellectuals collaborated to create environmentally friendly infrastructure that complemented nature.

As Eron explained his vision, holographic projections illuminated the stage, displaying creative designs that combined Solarian efficiency and Lunarian elegance. Green settings merge with metropolitan environments, showing the blend of contemporary technology and traditional traditions.

Eron's speech struck a deep chord with the audience, encouraging hope and fresh optimism about the future. He emphasised the value of inclusivity and collaboration, encouraging residents to actively shape the future of their community.

Aria stood by Eron's side, her eyes beaming with joy and admiration. She understood Eron's idea as more than just a design for infrastructure; it represented the triumph of unity over separation.

In the days that followed, Eron's vision ignited a surge of ingenuity and creativity throughout the city. Solarian and Lunarian craftspeople worked on public art projects that highlighted cultural variety, and engineers created cutting-edge technologies based on Lunarian ideals.

Eron established expert and community leadership groups to facilitate dialogue and collaboration on initiatives that promote sustainability and social fairness. They established the framework for a society in which development was defined not just by scientific breakthroughs, but also by kindness and empathy.

Eron's revelation marked a watershed moment in Aria's history, ushering in a future of Solarian creativity and Lunarian wisdom.

Chapter 25: The Rift

A ominous undercurrent undermined the fragile unity Aria and Eron had worked so hard to establish. A mysterious organisation, hidden in secret, sought to restart hostilities between the Solarian and Lunarian worlds, targeting Eron and Aria's ambitious efforts for harmony and growth.

Eron and Aria, unfazed by the impending threat, rallied their allies to discover the identities and motivations of the mysterious organisation. They ventured into the city's underworld, following vague indications and uncovering a web of deception that stretched over both the Solarian and Lunarian realms.

As tensions rose, Eron and Aria found themselves navigating a maze of intrigue and peril, their relationship tested by the rising threat of conflict. They drew on each other for support, pulling confidence from the unfailing love and unity that had kept them going through adversity.

Meanwhile, Aria's family played an important role in the inquiry, using Lunarian knowledge to provide light on the hidden organisation's ancient roots. Their knowledge of ancient prophecies pointed at a dark conspiracy that threatened to destabilise their society.

As Eron and Aria's world stood on the verge of catastrophe, they faced the dark organisation in a dramatic encounter that tested their ideals and determination. Aria stood by Eron's side, a quiet monument to the strength of unity in the face of suffering.

Chapter 26: Redemption

A shocking twist surfaced when Eron's estranged brother, long thought to be affiliated with the shadowy organisation, sought redemption by assisting Eron and Aria in foiling their malicious ambitions. The revelation created a sense of tension and hope as Eron and Aria navigated the complexities of family dynamics in the face of impending confrontation.

Eron's brother, formerly a symbol of separation and treachery, approached him, pleading for forgiveness and peace. His motivations remained a mystery, but Eron detected a real desire for redemption behind the surface.

Aria, ever the sympathetic soul, extended a hesitant hand of trust to Eron's brother, realising the possibility of healing and reconciliation within the chaos. They formed an uneasy collaboration in pursuit of a common goal: to expose the hidden organisation's evil objectives.

Eron struggled with mixed feelings as he confronted his brother's past transgressions, caught between doubt and a desire for family harmony. He grappled with the weight of betrayal and the prospect of forgiveness, aware that their joint future was at stake.

As tensions rose, Eron's brother offered crucial information that shed light on the clandestine organisation's inner workings. His insider knowledge was important in uncovering their malicious plots and foiling their intentions to create turmoil.

Aria's family expressed their support for Eron's brother, acknowledging the transformative power of redemption and compassion. Together, they forged an impressive alliance that overcame previous rivalries and divisions.

As the clandestine organisation's intentions collapsed, Eron's brother faced his past with courage and humility, seizing the chance for forgiveness. His trek paralleled the city's larger yearning for healing and harmony.

In a climactic encounter, Eron, Aria, and Eron's brother face the hidden organisation head on, their union serving as a sign of strength and optimism. They worked together to expose the organisation's goals and demolish its operations, clearing the way for a future of peace and collaboration.

Following the confrontation, Eron's brother accepted his role in crafting a better future for the Solarian and Lunarian worlds, his path to redemption demonstrating the transformational power of forgiveness and second chances.

Chapter 27: The Summit

Aria hosted a historic summit of Solarian and Lunarian officials, signalling a watershed point in the quest for unity and healing. The summit, conducted against the backdrop of societal transition and renewed hope, resulted in a historic pact of collaboration and mutual respect. Eron and Aria, Aria's visionary leaders, warmly welcomed dignitaries from both the Solarian and Lunarian realms, extending gestures of warmth and friendship. The city was buzzing with excitement and expectation as delegates came to discuss common challenges and goals.

The summit location, a large hall decorated with emblems of Solarian and Lunarian past, served as a tangible reminder of the solidarity they wanted. Delegates engaged in heated debates and talks, forming alliances that went beyond previous rivalries and divisions.

Aria's family was instrumental in fostering discourse and understanding, relying on Lunarian norms to bring harmony into the proceedings. Their thoughts and knowledge steered conversations toward consensus, setting the door for fruitful collaboration.

As tensions subsided and trust increased, Eron gave a moving speech emphasising the necessity of empathy and cooperation in creating a peaceful future. His comments hit home with the gathered leaders, motivating a shared resolve to reconciliation.

During the negotiations, Aria had genuine chats with her Lunarian counterparts, forming personal relationships that helped to bridge cultural gaps. Her empathy and compassion acted as a catalyst to foster trust and understanding.

Eron's influence on the Solarian council was essential in gaining concessions and accords that reflected Lunarian viewpoints. He expertly managed political issues, developing relationships and making compromises that established the framework for long-term cooperation.

Eron and Aria hosted a spectacular meal celebrating Solarian and Lunarian cultures, highlighting the richness of their shared ancestry, as a symbolic gesture of unity. The evening was full of music, dance, and laughing as delegates celebrated the spirit of friendship and good will.

As the conference concluded, Eron and Aria stood out as beacons of hope in a world torn apart by division. The treaty they forged was more than just a diplomatic triumph; it exemplified the transforming potential of unity and reconciliation in overcoming centuries of suspicion and hostility.

Chapter 28: Legacy

E ron and Aria's home was filled with excitement as they welcomed their first child into the world, symbolising the unification of the Solarian and Lunarian realms and heralding the promise of a happy future. The birth of their child restored hope and optimism in Aria, signalling the end of their road toward togetherness and reconciliation.

Aria's pregnancy had been a time of anticipation and reflection, with the city surrounding the expectant parents in love and support. Aria and Eron's enthusiasm grew as the day approached, and their hearts were filled with visions of a future where their child would grow up in peace and harmony. Aria gave birth in a beautiful location, surrounded by loved ones and midwives from the Solarian and Lunarian communities. Eron stood by her side, his face full of amazement and respect as he witnessed the miracle of new life.

Aria and Eron's hearts flooded with love and thankfulness when their baby was born, and their bond became stronger as they shared the joy of parenthood. They were impressed by the baby's looks, which were a wonderful blend of Solarian and Lunarian lineage.

In the days that followed, Aria ecstatically welcomed its newest resident. Celebrations and gatherings were arranged in honour of the child, emphasising the importance of their birth in the story of unity and reconciliation.

Aria's family incorporated traditional Lunarian traditions into the festive celebration. They poured blessings and presents on the child, expressing hope for a future in which cultural variety is acknowledged and valued.

Eron and Aria treasured quiet moments with their little one, relishing the magic of parenting and the prospect of a better tomorrow. Their love for each other became stronger as they embarked on this new chapter of their life, motivated by a common desire to leave a legacy of harmony and understanding.

As the city welcomed their kid as a symbol of hope and rejuvenation, Eron and Aria's legacy lived on, a tribute to love's transformational power in breaking down barriers and creating relationships across generations.

Chapter 29: Epilogue

Years later, after Aria and Eron's child was born, the world thrived thanks to their innovative leadership. Aria has grown into a beautiful example of unity and growth, with Solarian and Lunarian communities coexisting together, their cultures interlaced like threads in a beautiful tapestry.

Aria and Eron's child has grown into a caring and enlightened individual who embodies the merging of two worlds and carries on their parents' legacy of love and togetherness. The child's upbringing has been enhanced by exposure to both Solarian and Lunarian customs, fostering a strong awareness of cultural diversity and mutual tolerance.

As Aria and Eron gaze out upon the city they have helped construct, they are proud of the progress achieved toward reconciliation and understanding. Their love tale has become a treasured legend, passed down through generations as a source of hope and inspiration.

Aria and Eron's leadership has resulted in innovative policies that promote social fairness, environmental sustainability, and technological innovation. Solarian creativity and Lunarian wisdom continue to intersect, propelling progress and wealth throughout the region.

Aria's family continues to play an important role in promoting international conversation and collaboration, using their ancestral wisdom to bridge the gap between the past and the present. Festivals honouring Solarian and Lunarian customs have become signature events, attracting visitors from all around to witness the city's vibrant diversity.

Eron's brother, who has accepted forgiveness and reconciliation, plays an important position in Eron and Aria's administration as a trusted counsellor and advocate for togetherness. His journey from betrayal to atonement is lauded as a testament to the transformational power of second opportunities.

Eron and Aria's love for each other grows stronger with time, and their union serves as a pillar of strength in the face of governance responsibilities. They take quiet time together to reflect on their journey to this point and dream of a future in which their child inherits a world full of promise and possibilities.

Eron and Aria's legacy lives on in the hearts of Aria's residents, who remember their narrative through monuments and artworks that celebrate the triumph of love over division. The city's transformation into a symbol of unity demonstrates the enduring power of compassion and understanding.

Chapter 30: Reflections

Aria and Eron pause to reflect on their extraordinary journey, filled with gratitude for the strength of their love and the tenacity of their people. As they look at the city they helped create, they are struck with wonder and humility, marvelling at the astounding development made possible by teamwork and persistent dedication.

Aria and Eron sit together in a calm garden, surrounded by blooming flowers and soft breezes, reflecting on the struggles and successes that have characterised their road. They describe the difficulties they encountered—societal differences, political intrigue, and ominous threats—and how each hurdle only reinforced their determination to construct a better future.

Aria traces the lines on her child's face, a living monument to her and Eron's ambition of combining the Solarian and Lunarian worlds. She discusses the hope they held in their hearts, even throughout the darkest of circumstances, and how that hope flowered into concrete change.

Eron nods in accord, his eyes shining with pride as he looks at the cityscape. He describes periods of doubt and uncertainty, when the weight of leadership seemed overpowering, and how Aria's constant support served as his anchor throughout.

They honour the sacrifices made by their families, whose wisdom and counsel helped pave the ground for reconciliation. Aria's family, keepers of Lunarian tradition, had passed along ancient wisdom that enriched the city's cultural tapestry, whereas Eron's brother had found atonement in the search for unification.

Aria and Eron exchange anecdotes and laughs as they express gratitude for their people's tenacity in welcoming change with open hearts and minds. They remember communal gatherings, heated debates, and moments of collective celebration that deepened connection and solidarity.

In their observations, Aria and Eron understand the transformational power of love in breaking down barriers and building relationships. They discuss the common dreams they had fostered together, and how those dreams had blossomed into a shared reality that far exceeded their wildest expectations.

Aria and Eron renew their commitment to one other and their shared goal of a future ruled by compassion and empathy in the tranquil garden. They promise to continue their path toward oneness, confident that their love will guide them through the trials that lie ahead.

As the sun sets on their reflections, Aria and Eron take comfort in knowing that their narrative is far from over and that the legacy they have created together will continue to inspire future generations. With hearts full of hope and appreciation, they look forward to the future, knowing that their love will remain as a beacon of light in a world full of endless possibilities.

Chapter 31: Ever After

Aria and Eron stand side by side, looking out over the metropolis they've altered, as a new era dawns before them—a world where love knows no bounds and unity reigns supreme.

The air is thick with expectancy and excitement, echoing the heartbeat of a city transformed by solidarity, compassion, and fortitude.

Aria and Eron stand on a hill overlooking the city of Aria, bathed in the warm glow of the rising sun. The skyline is studded with constructions that combine Solarian innovation and Lunarian aesthetics, demonstrating their shared goal of peace and growth.

The couple's journey has been marked by spectacular highs and tragic lows, as well as trials that have tested and confirmed their love. Together, they have overcome treachery, battled prejudice, and broken down previously impenetrable boundaries.

Aria and Eron are joined in their reflections on their experiences by their adult kid, who represents hope and promise for the future. The youngster represents the unification of the Solarian and Lunarian worlds, a living testament to love's transformational power in bridging divides.

A quiet silence falls over the scene as a stunning spectacle unfolds in the skies above. Aria and Eron watch in astonishment as streaks of light dance over the horizon, painting the heavens in beautiful colours never seen before.

A quiet silence falls over the scene as a stunning spectacle unfolds in the skies above. Aria and Eron watch in astonishment as streaks of light dance over the horizon, painting the heavens in beautiful colours never seen before.

The display intensifies, dazzling the city in a kaleidoscope of colours that captures the hearts of its residents. Citizens congregate in the streets, their expressions filled with astonishment and joy as they watch the spectacular show.

Unbeknownst to Aria and Eron, the occurrence is actually a celestial celebration choreographed by the ancient Lunarian guardians, whose kind spirits have been watching over the city for generations. The guardians' ethereal presence exudes enchantment and regeneration.

As the performance reaches its climax, Aria and Eron share knowing glances, their hearts brimming with thanks for the love and unity that have guided them on their path. They clasp, their spirits bound together in a timeless embrace that transcends earthly boundaries.

In an unexpected but happy twist, a luminous figure emerges from the celestial display—a representation of the Lunarian guards themselves. The figure approaches Aria and Eron, offering a hand in a deep act of blessing and affirmation.

The guardians' presence gives Aria and Eron a sense of purpose and destiny, confirming that their love has surpassed mortal limitations and connected with cosmic powers beyond explanation. They are entrusted with the guardians' legacy, which will carry the spirit of togetherness and compassion forward for future generations.

Following the celestial festival, the city of Aria undergoes a significant shift, with its streets brimming with new vitality and excitement. The Solarian and Lunarian groups merge into a single civilization, with their distinctions cherished as sources of power and resilience.

Aria and Eron's legacy lives on as a light of hope and inspiration, with their narrative memorialised in songs and legends that reverberate throughout time. Their child develops into a leader with unmatched vision and empathy, passing on the torch of unity and understanding.

Happy, Aria, and Eron stand side by side, their hearts linked in a bond that spans time and place. Together, they look to the horizon, welcoming the dawn of a new era in which love knows no bounds—a tribute to love's enduring power to shape the fate of worlds.

ARIA TURNS TO FACE Eron, her eyes filled with unshed emotions of delight and thanks. "We did it," she says softly, her voice full of astonishment. "Against all odds, we've created a world where love knows no boundaries."

Eron smiles, his heart full of joy as he looks at the city he and Aria had helped transform. "Yes, my love," he says, his voice firm and emotional. "Together, we've shown that compassion and understanding can conquer even the deepest divisions."

THE END.

www.ingramcontent.com/pod-product-compliance
Lightning Source LLC
Chambersburg PA
CBHW070919160726
48004CB00003B/1430